THE AUTHOR'S LADY LIBRARIAN

A LAKE CHELAN NOVELLA

SHIRLEY PENICK

THE AUTHOR'S LADY LIBRARIAN

Copyright 2021 by Shirley Penick

THE AUTHOR'S LADY LIBRARIAN

is a work of fiction. All characters and events portrayed herein are fictitious and are not based on any real persons living or dead.

Photography by Jean Woodfin

Cover Models: Michelle Lynn McLeod and Darrin James Dedmond

Contact me:

www.shirleypenick.com

www.facebook.com/ShirleyPenickAuthorFans

To sign up for Shirley's Monthly Newsletter, sign up on my website or send email to shirleypenick@outlook.com, subject newsletter.

To Patty Anne Corder.
Thanks for being my very first super fan. It's so awesome to
have you in my corner.
Hope to see you in person again real soon!
Hugs and kisses.

CHAPTER ONE

Patty Anne LaGrange closed the book and put it back onto the bookshelf. It had been such an interesting book on Love Harbor in Massachusetts. Even though it was a book of history, the stories had been written as if they were fiction. She'd been sucked into stories of pirate ships crashing on the rocks near a whaling town, ships sinking, and sailors drowning. Even smugglers had roamed the shores to the point where the townspeople had hired a protector named Gideon McKeith a ruthless Scotsman with a huge broadsword studded in gems.

Patty Anne was so smitten with the stories she yearned to go visit the town. To keep ships from crashing into the rocks the town had built a lighthouse, three hundred years ago. She loved lighthouses, so it would be a delight to see. Maybe she would even be able to explore the caves and some of the original buildings. The graveyard would be fascinating to investigate to see where the great Scotsman was buried.

All the interesting things that she'd read about in the history book would come to life before her very eyes. She'd never been to the east coast. And as the town librarian, maybe it would be good if she expanded her horizons and experienced the eastern seaboard.

She had vacation time this summer. Normally she just stayed in Washington and enjoyed the surrounding mountains. But it was so tempting to think about going somewhere new.

Patty Anne wrestled with the idea. Should she, or shouldn't she? A traveling companion would make it more fun, but she didn't have one. It would be a bold move to go alone.

She pulled up the town website, which ridiculously boasted that true love was found by pilgrims seeking it. She rolled her eyes and wondered why the book she'd just read didn't have a whiff of that. Probably because someone less than fifty years ago had made it up. She wasn't the least bit interested in that foolishness. She scoured the pages trying to decide.

Finally, she asked herself, "Why not?" There was nothing holding her to this place for her vacation. She didn't have to stay in Washington State, or even Idaho. She could break out of her rut and go to the east coast. It would be fun to see Love Harbor and maybe some of the surrounding towns and states.

She had two weeks; she could probably see a lot of the area in that length of time. The states were so small over there, not like Washington, where it took a day to simply drive across, with no stopping to explore. She could maybe see three or four states.

She muttered, "That's not a bad idea. Maybe I should do that."

Patty Anne switched her web browser to the airlines. She would have to drive to either Spokane or Seattle. Taking the barge and then driving to one of the major cities would take one day each way. Still leaving her fourteen days because of the extra weekend.

She was surprised to find the costs from both airports to Boston weren't bad at all. She had plenty of money socked away. Her house was her family home, paid off long ago. Her car she'd purchased for the long haul and had paid it off last summer, so nearly all her salary went into savings and her vacation fund.

So, monetarily she was set. The time it took to fly across the country, on the other hand, was long. Over five hours each way. It would be an awfully long flight to be in the cramped seats of an airplane, not her idea of fun. She'd have to drive into Spokane or Seattle, the night before, and then catch an early bird flight to get her to the east coast by evening.

She talked herself into it. She was going to do it. With a deep breath she booked the flights, chose her seats, and started looking at rental cars and hotels. The more she explored, the more excited she got. Patty Anne LaGrange was going to be spending two glorious weeks on the East Coast. She could hardly wait.

The next step was to see if they had a library and connect with the librarian. An essential part of any visit was to have one local person as an acquaintance, and librarians were a tight knit family as well as helpful.

GIDEON ST. JAMES GLARED AT HIS COMPUTER SCREEN, THE blank white page, and the silently blinking cursor mocking him. It wasn't his computer's fault he couldn't write, of course, but he didn't have a mirror in his office so he couldn't glare at himself.

He was on deadline; this was *supposed* to be book three of a trilogy. Books one and two were already with his publisher. Now all he had to do was write book three. The problem was he'd killed off the planned hero of this book. It had needed doing but that left him with no clue as to what to do with book three. He didn't even have a character name to start with.

If he'd been a swearing type of man, he'd be cussing a blue streak, but his mother had forbidden coarse language. Even though she was gone now, he just couldn't go against her wishes. She'd washed out his mouth with soap so many times, the very idea of using a swear word made him a little sick to his stomach.

Making himself turn from thoughts of soap he fretted. He had to come up with names and a plot, and, well, everything. His publisher was not going to give a hoot that he had writer's block. Professional authors did not give into that luxury. They put their butts in the chair, their fingers on the keyboard, and wrote stories. Period. No excuses.

He wrote suspense, so all he needed was an inkling of an idea, to get him started. This particular series was based in Seattle, Washington. The first book, Taste of Poison, had been a murder at the Space Needle. His first thought was someone being pushed off the top, but that had been too ordinary. So, he'd made it a poisoning at the exquisite rotating restaurant. Making all the staff on duty that night suspects. He'd had a lot of fun with that one.

The second book, Splash of Poison, had been a drowning at the government locks, where the ships were raised and lowered between Puget Sound and Lake Washington. He knew Lake Washington sat twenty feet above sea level and was freshwater, compared to Puget Sound which was saltwater at sea level. He'd been fascinated by the locks after his visit to Seattle a few years ago. The murder he'd created had looked like an accident.

But the daughter of the victim had fought the authorities saying her father visited the locks once a month, was an excellent swimmer, and would have never gotten close enough to fall in. She'd argued that what with all the protective measures, it would take someone determined to die to get past them. She'd nagged and harangued them long enough; she'd felt like a fish wife. But they finally investigated it thoroughly, and had found a paralyzing poison as the culprit, as well as the person that had gotten her father past the protection.

Gideon stood to pace in front of his desk.

He just needed one more idea, a victim, a murderer, and some authority figures. He didn't want to use the same police, so he wanted it out of central Seattle and Ballard. Maybe somewhere east, or south.

Wracking his brain for an interesting location not too far from Seattle, he thought through different ideas. The duck tours maybe, but no that was still in Seattle. As was the football stadium, a murder at a game would be fun to write. The duck tours would be another drowning and he didn't want that.

Thinking further afield. Bellevue, he couldn't think of anything interesting other than maybe the light rail. Redmond had Microsoft but that didn't appeal. Following the idea of the light rail toward the south. Mount Rainier might work.

The gondola ride on Crystal Mountain to the restaurant at the top would be perfect. Drop of Poison could be the title.

He liked the idea. He started a brain dump of thoughts onto the blank page. This was it, what he'd been looking for.

CHAPTER TWO

$\mathcal{P}$atty Anne nearly danced into the airport. She was so darn excited to start her vacation. Technically it had started yesterday afternoon, when she'd driven her car onto the barge that would take her downlake to Chelan for the four-hour drive to Seattle.

There were flights out of Spokane, which was a shorter drive, but the trips from that airport all had a layover, so it was faster to drive into Seattle. Since it was summer, the sun didn't set until late in the evening, so she'd had plenty of time to reach Seattle and her hotel before nightfall.

She'd been up and ready, bright and early, left her car in long term parking, and had taken the shuttle to the airport. After going through security, she would be on her way.

Eight hours later, Patty Anne dragged herself off the plane. That had been the longest flight in history. She'd read books. She'd watched movies. She'd tried to nap. She'd even read the magazine in the back pocket of the chair in front of her, succumbing to doing the puzzles. But it still had been a horribly long flight.

Being on the aisle had been great for getting up occasionally, but that was all. Everyone walking by knocked into her, the food and drink service bumped her elbow. She'd been lucky to only have cool water splash on her when the plane hit a pocket of turbulence, much better than hot coffee, but...

The grumpy guy by the window was persnickety about everything. He was a short pudgy guy, balding on top with a ring of gray hair, he was dressed in a rumpled suit with his tie loosened. His looks were not the issue, it was his demands. "Just a little ice. No, one more cube." "Two napkins and an extra cup." "Did the snacks have gluten?" "Could he get a pillow and a blanket?" "His headset wasn't working very well." By the end of the flight Patty Anne and the stewardess had wanted to murder him, she was certain of it.

She'd gotten up a time or two just to stretch her legs on the long walk down the aisle to the bathroom. Not so much to even use it, but to just give herself the ability to move, and get away from her seat mate. It just hadn't helped that much. She'd eaten some of the food that was served, not because she was particularly hungry, but to give her a break in the monotony.

She was not a sit-around-and-do-nothing type of person, she liked to be up and busy. So being confined for that many hours, was just torture. She was finally in Boston, and she was ready to start her vacation. So even though she was tired and cranky, she wasn't about to let that ruin her time.

Patty Anne walked quickly through the airport, glad to be moving. When she got to the baggage claim, luggage was already coming down the ramp. People were gathering around to grab their own, her seat mate pushed his way through the pack.

Waiting patiently out of the line of fire, Patty Anne saw

hers come down the ramp, so she moved toward the end of the mob and when it came by, she grabbed it.

Her carry-on was quickly attached to the big suitcase and she tugged her purse strap across her body. Next stop, the shuttle to take her to the rental car lot. Of course, there was a line to get on the shuttle, and then once she got to the rental car place, there was another line. But she was on the ground, and she was standing. She was happy she wasn't sitting any longer.

When she got her car, she put all her luggage in the trunk, programmed the address of the hotel she was staying in tonight into the GPS and was off. She caught sight of a drive-through fish restaurant and couldn't help but stop and grab some fish and chips, they were a whole lot better than the food from the airplane.

Upon arriving at the hotel, she checked in, went upstairs, and took a shower. Traveling made her feel dirty and gritty, so she was glad to have a nice hot shower. She put on some cool pajamas and crawled into bed, then flipped the TV on to the local entertainment channel, so she could see what the hotel recommended for people on vacation to do.

They had lots of ideas, but nothing that really struck her. She might want suggestions later, but first, she wanted to go to Love Harbor and see it. She'd contacted the librarian, Jennifer, who had been warm and welcoming. Jennifer had been very enthusiastic about meeting with her and having a nice long chat about their libraries and their different locations.

Patty Anne decided to go to bed early so she could be on her way first thing in the morning. The hotel boasted a wonderful breakfast restaurant, and she was looking forward to trying some of the local favorites.

She was worried she wouldn't be able to sleep after being so bored on her flight. But that was not a problem. And her enthusiasm didn't cause any difficulty either, she drifted right off. The time difference got the best of her in the morning, however. Even though she'd gone to bed earlier than she normally would have at home. She still wasn't ready to get right up.

The three-hour time difference wasn't helpful, and she got moving later than she'd planned. But it was a vacation, so she didn't fret about it. She stretched luxuriously and reveled in the morning. A glance at the clock showed she needed to check out soon, so she got out of bed, packed up what she had gotten out from the night before, and took it all down to her rental car.

It took her a minute to find her rental, since there were lots of cars that looked just like hers, in the parking lot. She always wondered why rental vehicles were such nondescript colors. They were all tan or brown or gray and they looked like every other car in the lot. She would have made them red and blue and green, if she was in charge of rental cars. But she wasn't, so she'd had to find her brown car amidst the rest of the brown cars in the parking lot.

When she had her luggage safely stowed, she went back inside and checked out, then went to have breakfast. They had some wonderful-looking waffles. And she was trying to decide if she wanted those, or if she wanted something with a little more protein like an omelet. She flipped to the last page and saw a combo plate, that had both eggs, and a waffle. And that, she decided, was the one for her.

She happily ate her breakfast. Not quite finishing all of it, because there was a lot there, and she had several cups of coffee, too. Finally, she was ready to go on her way. She went back out, and again had to look for her rental car, she should have parked it in a specific spot, so it would be easy to find. But no, she hadn't.

Once she finally found it, again, the second time, she got in, put into the GPS the address of the library in Love Harbor, and was ready to go. It was quite a lovely drive, since she picked the scenic route rather than the fast route. She wanted to see everything she could, so she took a coastal road rather than the highway. It was so pretty.

Love Harbor was only a couple of hours from Boston. Even on the backroads, so she'd be there, about one. Which would give her librarian friend time to have lunch and then be back at her post. Patty Anne was so excited she felt like squirming in her seat.

She fought the urge, and drove along enjoying the view of the Atlantic Ocean, as opposed to the Pacific.

GIDEON STROLLED INTO THE LIBRARY. HE WANTED TO DO A bit more research. His publisher had loved his Seattle poison series, so they'd commissioned three more books. He'd decided to go further afield to eastern Washington. He'd asked Jennifer, the librarian, to get books on the area. They were on an inter-library loan.

When he'd gone to Seattle, he hadn't visited Eastern Washington. He thought about flying out to take a look himself, but it was a big area, so he wanted to investigate first, get some ideas of what to visit.

He'd requested travel books and history books and several different novels written about the area. He wanted some ideas of where he might place his murder mysteries. Once he'd ducked into the library he immediately went up to the desk, where Jennifer was chatting with a lovely lady, about his age, that he'd never seen before. She had a trim figure and long blonde hair pulled up in a ponytail. Glasses were tucked into the neck of her shirt and pulled the shirt a bit to gap open, he forced himself not to peek.

He waited until the librarian noticed him. Jennifer trilled, "Oh, Patty Anne, you need to meet Gideon. Gideon St. James is here to pick up some books about the area where you live."

"Gideon St. James? The murder mystery author? Really?'

Gideon nodded but didn't answer.

Patty Anne clapped her hands. "Are you going to write some stories in eastern Washington?"

Gideon didn't have the chance to answer. But he wasn't sure he could have. Patty Anne had dimples when she smiled. He loved dimples. Her brown eyes sparkled with joy and her made-for-kissing mouth was turned up in a grin.

Fortunately, Jennifer had jumped right in. "He is going to kill some people in eastern Washington, so he needs to research, for murder locations."

Patty Anne's eyes sparkled with excitement, drawing him in. She touched his arm, light as a feather. "Oh, you must put one in Chedwick. I'll tell you all about it then you'll know everything. Ooh, and another place that would be fun is Wenatchee. Hmm, you usually do trilogies. Isn't that correct?"

"Yes, I do."

She tapped a finger to her lips. "Leavenworth, or some of the southern cities like Yakima or Pasco or Walla Walla. I would be thrilled to tell you all about my part of Washington. Do you want to get together to talk while I'm here?"

He would love to spend some time with this delightful woman. He'd seen some of the cities she mentioned and would never have pronounced their names the way she did, but he'd found that to be true when he'd visited Seattle.

"That would be excellent. Thank you for such a generous offer."

"I love your books, I'm happy to help."

Jennifer leaned on the counter. "She's a librarian too. Just like me, so she's read all your books."

"Well, maybe not exactly all of them, but many of them, especially the more recent ones," Patty Anne said with a smile. "I read a book about the history of Love Harbor. Are you the one that wrote it? The author's first name was Gideon, the last name was different. But your writer's voice came through, at least I thought so."

Gideon smiled. Most people didn't associate his history book with his murder novels. "Yes, I did. I'm a descendant of one of the founding families. So, I figured since I've heard the stories all my life, I should make a nice little history book on the area." He shrugged. "Even though it ended up being more of a novel than a history book."

One of the founding families? She thought he was being modest; she'd bet her last dollar he was a descendant of the protector Gideon McKeith. "It was awesome. In fact, that's why I'm here. When I read it, I felt drawn to come visit and explore." Patty Anne held her hands out to encompass the whole area.

"Well, thank you. So, would you like to have dinner with me this evening?"

"Oh, that would be wonderful."

She hadn't hesitated but he wondered if she would be more comfortable with others in attendance. He turned to Jennifer. "Do you want to come too, Jennifer? And Jerry, if he's off."

"No, you two have fun. Jerry is off and we have a date planned around Netflix."

Gideon's face heated.

Patty Anne asked, "Is that a euphemism for…"

Jennifer laughed. "No, there really is a show we've been waiting to watch; Jerry so seldom gets a night off. Although we might chill after we watch it." She gave them a sly grin.

He held up his hand like a stop sign. "TMI."

Jennifer turned back to Patty Anne. "We'll catch up later."

Patty Anne nodded, "Sure thing. You have to give me some suggestions about where to go and what to see."

Jennifer chuckled, "Gideon can do that just as well as I can."

Patty Anne looked at him then back to Jennifer and lowered her voice. "Well yes, but he is a guy."

Jennifer guffawed. "True. He is a guy."

He didn't know whether to be insulted or relieved he was off the hook for touristy things.

Patty Anne pulled her purse off the counter. "Well, I'm gonna go check into my Bed and Breakfast. I came straight here to meet you, Jennifer. I still need to check-in."

"I feel so honored you came here first."

Gideon was glad he'd managed to arrive at the right time. He was looking forward to spending time with the lovely Patty Anne.

Patty Anne held out her hand to him. "Nice to meet you, Gideon." She hugged Jennifer. "And you can get his books all checked out."

Jennifer put her hands on her hips. "You are taking her to the Dolphin Run Tavern, aren't you? It is the most iconic place in all of Love Harbor."

Did Jennifer think he was a moron? "Of course. Patty Anne, how about I pick you up at six-thirty?"

"How will you know where I am?"

Like there were a thousand choices in Love Harbor, he

could walk between the two they did have. "We don't have a lot of B&Bs in town. Johnson or Sheridan?"

Patty Anne laughed. "Sheridan."

Her laugh skittered through him, nearly rendering him speechless. "Excellent. See you then."

She nodded and sashayed out the door. Like a statue he watched her go. It was going to be an interesting night.

CHAPTER THREE

*P*atty Anne was excited, and also a little nervous about going to dinner with Gideon St. James. She was a huge fan of his writing, so she was a little in awe of him. His looks had also drawn her in, he was strong and muscly, almost like a bodybuilder. His short gray hair and trimmed beard framed brown eyes and a strong face.

She'd met authors before; he wasn't her first one. But he was probably one of the biggest authors she'd met, not counting Jeremy Scott who lived in their town and wrote children's stories. Gideon was an awesome author, almost always hitting the best sellers list. She enjoyed his stories so much, even though they were a little on the bloody side.

Well not bloody exactly, but they did have a lot of murder. She chuckled at herself. He was a murder mystery author so that wasn't a surprise. His last three books had been based in Seattle, and surrounding areas, and had all dealt with poison. Now he was working on another trilogy. She speculated if he was still going to do the poison aspect, or whether it was going to be a new type of death that he was going to use for this trilogy.

After her shower, she dressed in a pretty turquoise sleeveless shirt, with a white ruffle edging the scoop neckline, and a pair of black slacks. Nothing fancy, but pretty enough to go anywhere. She didn't know what the dress code was at the Dolphin Run Tavern, probably casual, but she didn't want to be too casual just in case it was a little more upscale than its name indicated. Love Harbor wasn't exactly a tourist town, even with the true love hook. They had a few amenities and a few attractions. Not anything like Chedwick which had a very definitive bent towards attracting tourists. Both towns had a similar population size.

Patty Anne hoped she could get Gideon to open up about being the descendant of the protector the town had hired. She wondered if he still had the broadsword, wouldn't that be fun to see!

Arriving in the front parlor to wait for him, she saw a few other people that were also staying at the B&B. She nodded to them, being friendly without engaging, since Gideon would be arriving at any moment.

She went over to the door and looked out the window. It was a lovely front door with skinny floor-to-ceiling windows on both sides of the door, with sheer shimmering lace-edged curtains over them, and a lovely glass inset of the lighthouse. The perfect decor for what one would think of in this area of the eastern seaboard.

Moments later, Gideon walked in the door. He was such a good-looking man, slightly taller than her and distinguished, his hair trimmed on the sides and a little longer on top. He was dressed casually in slacks and a polo shirt.

Patty Anne breathed a sigh of relief that she'd picked the right outfit. Not too fancy. Not too casual. He grinned when he saw her, and she smiled back, feeling a little flustered by her reaction to his smile. She walked over to him as he walked to her, meeting in the middle.

"Are you ready?" he asked.

"I am. I have lots of questions, I'm going to ask you know."

"The life of an author. I would expect nothing less. Let's go."

She walked out and he held her door so she could slide into his Lexus. She'd questioned if he would come roaring up in a Lamborghini or something else expensive and flashy. But no, if he had those cars, he'd left them at home and come in quiet luxury.

It wasn't far to the Dolphin Run tavern. Nothing was very far away in this little town. Two streets held stores and shops, while the rest of the streets were homes. There was a two-mile drive to the lighthouse and she definitely wanted to see that tomorrow.

He pulled up in front of the Dolphin Run. It was charming, one of the older buildings in town, obviously, built back when the town first was getting started, which meant it was much larger than most of the other buildings. She guessed there might be living quarters above the tavern.

Patty Anne took Gideon's arm as he escorted her in the door. She enjoyed him playing the gentleman. They were both of an age where it was a sign of respect for him to open doors and treat her like a lady, and she was perfectly happy with that.

GIDEON HAD TO HOLD HIS SIDES FROM LAUGHING SO MUCH. Patty Anne had a sly sense of humor and the delivery had caught him off guard every time. His face hurt from too much smiling.

They'd had a wonderful dinner of locally caught fresh fish and an ale brewed nearby. She'd given him lots of information on the area she lived in and he had multiple ideas for his new stories. He would take his ideas back and research the areas more. Her amusing tales had been mostly about the shenanigans in her hometown. But a few had been from trips to neighboring towns.

She sat back and said, "Your turn."

"My turn?"

She pointed at him with the dessert spoon. She'd had chocolate mousse and watching her lick that spoon with each bite had about driven him crazy. He'd tried to focus on anything but that, but he'd been sucked in, the rest of the restaurant was just too familiar. She, on the other hand, was fascinating. "Yep. Start talking."

He shook his head. "I don't have any funny stories."

"I want to hear about the history of Love Harbor. Not what's in the book, but little tidbits you left out."

He frowned, wracking his brain for the stories he'd heard his whole life and things he'd left out of the book.

After he was silent for several minutes, she said. "Start by telling me about the caves. Did you explore them as a child?"

"Naturally. Every single kid from Love Harbor explored them, except maybe some of the girls, that actually believed the ghost stories."

"I don't recall ghost stories in the book."

"That's because they were made up simply to keep us kids from exploring the caves and getting lost or hurt. Of course, for most of us it made us want to go even more."

She grinned. "Obviously."

He waggled his eyebrows. "When we got older, we used the stories to get the girls into our arms by pretending we heard a scary noise. I don't think the girls were scared, but they didn't hesitate to go along with our shenanigans."

Her eyes twinkled. "I imagine they were glad for an excuse to cuddle up. Did any of them ever pretend they heard a scary noise and needed your protection?"

He couldn't stop the grin from spreading across his face. "A time or two, yes."

She laughed. "Tell me some of the ghost stories."

He settled in to do just that. "Captain Black was a particularly scary fellow. He was a pirate, a murderous sort. When he captured other ships, he would give that crew one chance to sign on as one of his gang and if they didn't, he filleted them and fed them to the sharks. When he crashed on the Love Harbor shore, rumors spread that he was continuing his murderous ways, hiding in caves, and searching for the treasures he lost when his ship ran aground. No one went near the caves for fear of him killing them. Shark sightings took an upturn as well. Years later people swore he was still inhabiting the caves."

Patty Anne shuddered dramatically. "Is that why the town brought in the ruthless Gideon McKeith?"

Gideon gave her a sly smile then continued to talk about different pirates and ghosts for nearly an hour. His throat stopped him from going even longer. It was dry as a bone. He glanced around and noticed only one other table was occupied. He figured the staff would like to get some sleep. "I think we've worn out our welcome," he said quietly.

Patty Anne looked around. "I think you're right."

He left a large tip and the two of them left the restaurant part of the Tavern. "Do you want to go into the honky-tonk?"

She yawned. "Not tonight. I shouldn't be so tired because of the time difference, but I am."

"Travelling can really take it out of you, especially clear across the country." He steered her toward his car.

"Sad but true."

"We could meet up tomorrow and I could take you to the lighthouse and go beyond to see the first cave or two." He had no idea why he'd offered to do that, other than he'd enjoyed her company.

"I don't want to be a burden. I know you have work to do."

"The beauty of being my own boss is I decide when to write. I'll probably jot down some of the ideas you gave me tonight and be ready to ask more questions tomorrow."

"Oh, well in that case, if I'm helping, yes, I would enjoy you showing me the lighthouse and some caves."

"Excellent, eleven and we can get lunch? Or one, after lunch?"

"Let's do after. I want to check out some shops in the morning. I heard of one called Treasures of the Deep."

"Oh yes, Martie has lots of fun items, all found in the ocean. She scuba dives to collect them." He pulled up in front of her temporary home.

"So, I'll go shopping and meet you, where at one?"

"We can meet here at your B&B, so you can store your treasures before we go off exploring."

"Perfect. Thank you for a wonderful evening."

"The pleasure was all mine." She went in the door and he thought maybe he should have kissed her cheek.

With a sigh, he went home and spent several more hours plotting out his next three books, which actually ended up being ideas for six. It took him so much longer than it normally would have, because his mind kept drifting back to the lovely woman he'd had dinner with. And his regrets for not kissing her on the cheek or even her luscious mouth, had doubled the time he normally would have needed. Tomorrow couldn't come fast enough.

atty Anne slept a little later than she'd planned, her body was still confused by the time change. She did manage to make it to the breakfast room before they closed it up for the morning. The coffee and enormous banana nut muffin were the perfect start for her day, she had a small scoop of fruit with it and took an orange for later, in case she needed it.

Her first stop was going to be Treasures of the Deep; she was so excited to see what the proprietor had found at the bottom of the ocean. So many ships had crashed along these shores, before the lighthouse was established, that she supposed there might be all kinds of interesting things to find.

Treasures of the Deep was a delight, she could hardly stand still, she wanted to see everything at once. On the walls there were wooden planks, ship wheels, and nets strung. Framed newspaper articles hung on the walls, looking closely she realized they were all about famous shipwrecks. There were lots of shells strewn about, intermingled with treasures.

Glass cases held expensive, and, she assumed, rare items. Other tables held coins that were more weathered than those in the cases. Old fashioned lanterns gave off a soft glow. A soothing rhythmic sound of the tide and a clanging bell filled the room with just the right amount of background noise.

Each area had a theme, one was all about money found, gold and silver coins aplenty with a few different designs, some had been turned into pendants. She wondered if they were the pieces of eight, she'd heard about in pirate movies.

Another section was pottery, plates, bowls, tea pots, and small containers, some with lids, and some without. She wasn't quite sure what they would have been used for. There were pretty chains with pendants made of coins and other jewelry, earrings, rings, and bracelets.

Swords and an anchor were mounted or tucked in a corner, they were corroded from the salt water, but it was clear what they had been. Patty Anne was drawn to the glass cases that had coins in them, some of which had been set in a bezel for wearing as a pendant.

When the proprietor finished with the customer she'd been working with, when Patty Anne had walked in the door, she came over and greeted her. "Hi, I'm Martie Deep. This is my shop. What do you think so far?"

"I think it's quite fun," Patty Anne said. "I was wondering, are these gold coins pieces of eight?"

Martie grinned. "No pieces of eight are silver, and they are from Spain, they were basically a Spanish dollar and represented eight reals, so to make change they could be cut into eight pie-shaped pieces. These are gold from several different countries. I have some silver coins, but still no pieces of eight."

Patty Anne struggled not to be disappointed. "Oh, okay. They're so pretty."

"They are. Did you like the ones you can wear?"

"I do, I'm going to get one. And I'm going to get a couple

of others for some friends." She glanced over at the loose coins on the table. "I also want to have some kind of a contest and give some trinkets away to some children. Or maybe some adults as well. I'm always trying to encourage more reading."

"Are you a librarian?" Martie asked.

She beamed at the woman's intuition. "I am, in a little town in eastern Washington State."

"Oh, my. You've come quite a distance."

"I have. I read a book about the history of the area and it was so well told, I just wanted to come see it."

"The book Gideon wrote, I'll bet."

"Yes. I didn't know it was his, of course, because he used a pen name on it. As opposed to his murder mysteries, or maybe it's the other way around. Maybe he used his real name on the history book, and his murder mysteries are under his pen name."

"No, his real name is Gideon St. James, the pen name he used for the history book is his first name and his mother's maiden name."

"Oh, well, that's nice, a way to hide in perfect sight." Patty Anne glanced around the store. "I don't see a single mention of the legend of meeting your true love after visiting *Love Rock*."

"That's because it's a crock of crap some over-eager town newbie started about fifty years ago. It's not in Gideon's book either."

"No, but I had to ask."

"We had to reincorporate the town as Love Harbor, rather than Lovington Bay. Many were ticked off by that, but money talks."

Patty Anne could understand the sentiment. "Did it help, this still doesn't seem to be much of a tourist destination."

"It probably helped at first, but you're right we aren't touristy. Only a few things of interest, so it ends up being a day trip for most people."

"Yeah only two B&Bs probably has something to do with that." Before Martie got any more upset Patty Anne decided to find a new area to talk about. "Changing the subject. So, any ideas to entice kids to read more."

"Well I would say a sword for the boys, but that's probably not appropriate. Maybe a little bag of coins or a treasure box, you can probably buy a small box that looks like a treasure box. And then fill it with some coins, maybe some chocolate coins as well. So that they have both a treat, and some historic coins."

"That's a great idea, kids always go for chocolate. As long as the real coins aren't too expensive, I could give a few of them out at different levels. Even the adults would probably enjoy that."

"Yeah, they might. I like chocolate, don't you?" Martie asked with a chuckle. "We can look at your budget and fix you up."

"Thanks."

"So, you came all this way just to see our little town?"

"I did, and I just happened to bump into Gideon in the library. I had gotten in touch with Jennifer, and we built up a little bit of a relationship over the months before I could get here. So, I stopped by to see her first and who was there, but him, picking up library books and history books of the very area I live in."

Martie nodded. "Ah, he's starting a new series, is he?"

"He appears to be, yes. In eastern Washington."

"That makes sense. His last one was in Seattle, western Washington, I guess he's still interested in the area."

"Apparently. Our side of the state would be happy to have

some fictional murders take place. But he doesn't know that much about eastern Washington, so we're spending a little bit of time together. I can tell him things and in exchange, he can spill some of the goodies that he didn't get to put in the book."

"Oh, that's fun. I'm sure there will be a few of those. Although I have to warn you, he's a better storyteller on paper than he is verbally."

Patty Anne wasn't sure she agreed with that, he'd done a good job last night, at least in her opinion. "We're gonna go up and look around the caves a little bit as well. Maybe this afternoon."

"That sounds like fun. Don't believe the ghost stories."

Patty Anne laughed. "He told me all about them last night and the pranks the boys pulled on the girls when they turned into teenagers."

"Yeah, well they sure did try, but most of the girls only fell for it when they wanted to."

"That does not surprise me in the least." She picked up a small porcelain bowl. "What were these little bowls for?"

"We have to speculate because I don't know for sure. I would think maybe snuff or incense."

Patty Anne turned the one she held in her hand, it seemed so delicate. "It's amazing how things can live under the sea for a couple of centuries, isn't it? I'm surprised the waves didn't break them up."

Martie shook her head. "There are no waves at the bottom, the waves are at the top. Unless there's fish in there poking around, there wouldn't be anything to disturb them."

"I guess I didn't think of that. So, you scuba dive down to get these trinkets?"

"I do. I found out about a particular ship that sank. And I managed to find it, and I've been bringing up some of the treasures from it. Everything in this shop I personally found. I don't buy from anyone else. I go down alone and bring up my finds."

Patty Anne shivered; she couldn't imagine going to the depths of the ocean alone. "You have fun with that."

Martie laughed. "I do, it's enjoyable, scary sometimes down there by myself, but exciting."

"Yeah, I'm not sure I would want to go down alone, maybe with a couple of other people, it would be fine."

"Do you scuba dive?"

"No, I never have."

"It's really a fun thing to do. You should try it. These days if you get a good company, they give you all the instructions and help you with all the information that you need to know to go down with them."

"Maybe I will try it someday, seems like it would be kind of cold up here."

"Oh yes, you have to have a wetsuit otherwise you would freeze right into a popsicle."

"I don't think I'd want to be a shark's popsicle."

"No, me either. I have an exceptionally fine wetsuit, two actually."

Patty Anne noticed the time on an old clock by the cash register. "Changing the subject, where's a good place to eat for lunch? That's kind of speedy, I need to meet Gideon at one o'clock. And I got a little bit of a late start. I didn't get to go quite as many places as I had thought, but this was my primary focus for this morning. It's the shop I wanted to come to the most."

Martie grinned. "We do have unique items for sale. For lunch, I think if it was me, I'd go to the Lobster Hut. It's not far away, only a couple of buildings over. And it's a casual place, you can get your food to go or you can go in and sit down. Either one."

"It might be fun to buy a lobster."

"They do sell them, but then you have to have somewhere to put them and cook them. I'm not sure the B&B would be down with that idea. If you let the Lobster Hut do the cooking, you can either get it as a whole lobster and pick out all the meat, or they've done that for you and you can just get a nice little sampler of it, or even a lobster taco."

What intriguing menu choices. "That sounds interesting, a lobster taco."

"They're incredibly good, get at least two, if you only get one, you'll be sorry, trust me on that. They're delicious."

"I will. That's a great idea. Thank you."

"Well, let me ring you up so you can get going, you don't want to miss Gideon."

"Thanks." Patty Anne picked out a few more items and added them to her pile. One of the little bowls. That would be her own particular treasure, as well as the necklace. "Can I wear the necklace?"

"Of course."

She pulled it out. There was a mirror nearby for people that wanted to do the same thing she was doing, she looked into it, it looked so pretty on her.

"Thank you so much. I might come back before I leave the area. I'm going to be here two weeks."

"That's a nice long time for a visit."

"Well, if I'm going to come all the way across the country that takes two days to get here. I need to use the time."

Martie's eyebrows rose. "Two days? Why two days?

"Our little town is so remote; you have to take a ferry. A walk-on ferry. Or you can put your car on a barge and take it down the first day, and then drive to Seattle. After you get off the ferry or the barge, and spend the night, then you have to take the early bird flight out in the morning to get here at a reasonable hour."

"Oh my. That is quite a chore isn't it."

"Yes, it is, but it's a wonderful place to live. So, I'm not going to complain about it. In fact, I'm used to it. Every summer for my vacation. I get out of town and go somewhere, sometimes it's close. Sometimes it's not so close. This is the farthest I've ever gotten though."

"Well, you can't get much farther except maybe Florida."

"True. I'll probably see you again Martie, it was nice to meet you."

"Nice to meet you as well Patty Anne, come back anytime."

GIDEON LOOKED AT THE CLOCK. IT WAS ONLY ELEVEN THIRTY. He had an hour and a half to wait to meet up with Patty Anne. He wondered if she'd gotten a lot of shopping done.

He'd been up late into the night, or into the morning actually, drafting out six different story ideas he'd come up with after talking to her yesterday. This morning when he'd gotten up, he'd gone back and examined them, and he still liked them. He'd either have to drop it down to three or talk his publisher into doing a six-book series. He'd always done trilogies, but maybe a longer series would be fun.

He could work on fleshing them out and see if any of them dropped out of their own accord. That happened sometimes. When he had a bit of an idea but not a fully-fledged one that could be turned into a complete story.

Gideon had gone for a jog to clear his brain and give his body some exercise, writing was a sedentary occupation and he had to remind himself to keep moving. He'd taken a leisurely shower, letting his mind float, he kept water-proof notes and a pencil handy in case his mind wanted to think about story ideas. He was certain every single author on the planet got some of their best ideas in the shower.

However, his mind, today, had been occupied by Patty Anne, not the stories. She was a pretty thing, but that was only part of the attraction. She had a brilliant mind, as a historian, a librarian, and a comedian. He'd never laughed so much in his life as he had yesterday. He was ready to go meet up with her again, and it wasn't even noon. If he knew where she was going to go for lunch, he would meet her there, or just happen to drop by. He shook his head, stalker much?

He marched over to the fridge telling himself he needed to leave the poor woman alone for five minutes. He had plenty of food to eat at home. He yanked open the fridge and glared inside. "Well, shoot." The emptiness of his refrigerator nearly echoed his words back to him.

There was a bag of now-slimy salad. Two eggs, something that might have once been bacon, but was dried out and curled up on the ends and was a funny color. An empty wrapper of cheese slices mocked him, as did the dried-up orange and single carrot in the fruit and vegetable drawer.

He slammed the door shut and heard the few containers of condiments rattle together. An enormous note, on the front of the freezer part, yelled out BUY GROCERIES!!!!! He needed a keeper, no doubt about it.

He thought back to the idea of lunch with Patty Anne. She'd said she was going to go to Treasures of the Deep. And if he knew Martie… Martie would suggest the Lobster Hut. It was one of her favorite places to go. And it had darn good food in his opinion. The lobster tacos were actually the best, ever.

Maybe if he just happened to go by there and get a couple of tacos.

And if Patty Anne was there, because Martie had sent her there, all the better. He pulled on his shoes and a jacket and went out the door. Normally he would walk to the Lobster Hut, but since they were going to go exploring further afield, he took his car. When he walked in, he spotted her immediately. She was sitting at a little two top and was indeed looking excitedly at lobster tacos.

He meandered over, ignoring the tank of lobsters and the others ordering from the takeout counter. "Mind if I join you?"

She glanced up and a wide smile covered her face. "Not at all, feel free. Martie suggested I come here."

"They do have darn good food, that's for sure."

She took a big bite and moaned in appreciation. "These are to die for. She said I should only get two tacos, but I'm thinking maybe I need three they are so good."

He nodded. "Well, one is never enough. Two is actually the sweet spot. Three and you start getting a little too full."

The waitress came up and he said, "I'll have three lobster tacos. And some iced tea."

Patty Anne guffawed. "You said only get two!"

He nodded solemnly. "Yes, but I'm a growing boy."

"That's not fair."

He continued on like she hadn't spoken. "Besides, I'll share it with you if you still want more."

Her eyes lit. "Oh. In that case, go right ahead and order three, Gideon."

"Your wish is my command, madam."

She gave him a little smirk that he wanted to kiss off her lips. "In that case, I'll have to think of more wishes."

He needed to get his mind off her lips, immediately. "What did you buy? That necklace maybe?"

She preened. "I did. Isn't it pretty?"

His voice softened as he was pulled into her sphere. "Yes, it is." He cleared his throat and did a mental head shake, pulling out of the vortex. "What else did you get?"

"Some trinkets for people at home, and a clever, I think, incentive for having children read more. I think I'm going to have some tiny treasure boxes made and fill them with chocolate candy coins and a few of the real coins from the store."

"Oh, that would capture a kid's interest, for sure. Maybe even an adult."

"That thought did cross my mind. What did you do while I was out shopping?"

He wasn't about to tell her his major focus of the morning, since it had been her. "I outlined some story ideas from what you told me last night. I have six."

Her eyebrows shot up. "Six? You usually write trilogies, don't you?"

"Yes, I do. I'm going to flesh them out a little more and see if any of them die. And if they don't, I'll talk to my publisher about doing my first six books series."

Patty Anne clapped her hands. "Oh, that would be fun, especially about my home area."

He chuckled at her enthusiasm. "You did a good job on selling it yesterday."

"I did, didn't I?" Her eyes sparkled with mirth.

"Whew. You're quite the card, aren't you?"

"Yes, I am. I'm precocious."

He raised one eyebrow. "Usually that's a term for children."

She shrugged. "Yeah, usually."

He chuckled. "Well, precocious on."

"I will."

The waitress set his tacos down in front of him with a nice large glass of sweet tea. And he dug right in.

Patty Anne had consumed her second taco, before he finished his first one, and she was eyeing his plate. He pretended not to notice to let her stomach weigh in on that decision. He would be happy to share, if she had the room.

By the time Gideon finished his second taco, she was sitting back a little more relaxed.

"So, do you want some of my third taco?"

She shook her head sadly. "No, I'm actually feeling pretty full… Maybe one bite."

He laughed and cut her a generous portion. "Here you go."

She snapped the food into her mouth. "It's just so delicious."

"Well, there's nothing stopping you from coming here every day for lunch."

She sighed. "I'm sure there's other things I need to taste in the area too."

He grinned at her morose attitude, then teased. "Probably, but these are good."

"They are. I love them. Maybe I'll do every other day."

He worked hard not to laugh. "That's a good compromise."

CHAPTER FIVE

*P*atty Anne looked around the room, there wasn't anything else to eat or drink, their plates were clean, and she was a little past full, it was time to go exploring. "Are you ready to go? I can't wait to see the lighthouse. I saw it last night when we went to the Dolphin Run for dinner. But just the light, not the actual lighthouse, that I could touch and feel and explore. I can hardly wait."

He shook his head at her silliness. "Absolutely ready, now's a perfect time to go." He signaled the waitress and handed her his credit card.

Patty Anne had not even had a chance to pay. "You don't always have to foot the bill, you know."

"I was raised to be the one that paid. Besides, I'm a world-famous author, you know. I can't have my fans thinking I'm a cheapskate."

Patty Anne laughed. "All right. If you insist, Mr. World-famous Author."

He stood and spied the many bags surrounding her. "So, do you want to take all your purchases back to the bed and breakfast first, so we don't have to worry about them in the car?"

"That would be wonderful. Thank you."

They both had at least four huge bags that weighed nearly nothing. Martie, was a wrapping maniac, nothing of hers was going to get broken.

He opened the car door for Patty Anne, took her packages and put them along with the ones he carried in the backseat. "It looks like you had a fine time at Treasures of the Deep."

"I did. Martie has so much information. And such cool things."

He drove the few blocks. "She does."

"Stay in here and wait for me, those bags weigh next to nothing."

"Martie does love her paper."

"I may have to buy a new suitcase just to get them back home."

He thought about her returning home while she ran her purchases into the bed and breakfast, he was going to miss her when she left. He'd known her less than twenty-four hours and knew that was true. Stupid, but true. He would remember her as he wrote his novels about eastern Washington.

She was back in the car before another thought could form, but something niggled.

He said, "All right, let's go see your lighthouse."

"Yay!"

Gideon drove down the road, past the Dolphin Run, over the bridge, she saw the lighthouse next to the shore.

"There it is," she gasped.

"Yes."

"It's kind of pretty but could use a coat of paint."

"No one's painted it in a few years. People don't live at the lighthouse anymore. It's all electronic now. When people lived here, they painted it regularly."

She frowned at him. "It should have a nice facelift. I think there is a local author who lives here that should drum up people to do that."

Gideon jerked. "Me? I'm not exactly a social person. Most writers aren't you know, they tend to stay to themselves and be introverts."

"You have not acted very introverted to me."

"No, you captured my attention the first moment. Your enthusiasm for everything sucked me right in. Plus, you're a very pretty lady."

PATTY ANNE GLOWED FROM THE PRAISE. SHE'D BEEN attracted to Gideon from the first moment as well. But she had been pushing it aside. Now that she heard that he felt, at least something similar, maybe she would stop pushing it to the side. And let nature take its course. Not that they were going to have a long-standing relationship, she was only here for two weeks, and lived on the completely opposite side of the country. But she could have fun for a few days with the man if he was willing. A long-distance relationship with a famous author? Nope, not happening.

She wasn't ready to make any decisions about that this instant, so she said, "Can we go up in the lighthouse?"

"If someone is here to let us in or if they are having tours," he said looking around. "There might be someone here."

Patty Anne had noticed an old bicycle leaning against the building near a door. Was that what he was referring to?

"I don't know whether they're having tours today or not. Like I said, it's fully automated now so people don't live here, but they do come out, to let tourists go up and see what it looks like. Usually on the weekend. There is also a museum set aside where you can see the workings from the past. Maybe we should have called and let them know we'd like to come out. But we're here now, so we'll see."

"I don't see any cars."

"No, but that bicycle looks like Jimmy's. If he's here, we're in luck."

"Oh, goody."

After parking, they got out of the car, there was a light breeze with the smell of the ocean all around them. Seagulls swooped overhead, diving just on the other side of what she assumed were cliffs. No one came out to greet them when they walked up to the lighthouse, so he knocked on the door and rang the bell next to it.

A tall, lanky, young man with red spiky hair, and a scraggly moustache answered the door. "Hey Gideon, what's up?"

"Jimmy, my friend here, would like to see the inside. Are you giving tours today?"

"I wasn't planning to. I'm doing a little maintenance. But there's no reason why you can't show her around."

"If you don't mind, I can do that. It's not like I haven't been here a few times," Gideon said in a sarcastic sounding tone of voice.

The guy, Jimmy, laughed. "True that man, true that. Okay, I'll let you get to it. Have fun. Let me know when you leave, so that I don't lock you in."

"That wouldn't be too much fun."

"No, it wouldn't, later."

Jimmy meandered off and Gideon turned to her. "Ready?"

"You betcha," she said in her best New England accent.

Gideon just laughed. "Let's go up first, so we get the strenuous part of the tour in first."

"Also, the most fun."

"Undoubtably. I'll bring up the rear. If you start feeling dizzy or winded just stop and take a moment. It's a long way up."

She laughed. "You'll have to come see my library some time. But I'll keep your advice in mind."

GIDEON HAD NO IDEA WHAT SHE'D MEANT BY THAT statement, but climbing the eight-story spiral staircase was not the time to ask, or talk. The staircase hugged the outside wall and was wide enough for an adult. It had a handrail both on the outside and one attached to the wall. It was safe enough as long as a person didn't get dizzy from going around in circles, or tired from too much climbing. He took the rear in case she wobbled, he could steady her, provided he didn't become mesmerized by watching her sweet derriere climb each step. He'd just set himself up for pure torture, sweet, but still torture.

As they climbed and climbed and then climbed some more, he thought about visiting her library. A trip to eastern Washington could certainly be used as a research trip, since three to six of his next books would take place in that region. He had every intention of putting one in her town, so a trip to see it firsthand would be reasonable. Then touring some of the other locations he had in mind would be a natural extension, as well as a pleasant holiday.

He wouldn't mind seeing her again after she'd gone back. He wanted to spend as much time with her in his hometown as he could. He could easily count it as research also. Wasn't he getting clever with the use of his time and excuses for it?

When they finally reached the top, he was glad for the benches where they could rest and also see out. It was a gorgeous view. He pushed one of the windows open a little to let in the breeze and the sound of the waves crashing on the rocks.

"Oh, Gideon, that view is amazing. I got my exercise for the day on those stairs. Mouthing off about my library that's only four stories when this is easily double that. But worth every step." She fanned herself with her hand. Patty Anne's eyes sparkled with enthusiasm for the views of both the ocean and back toward town. A person could see for miles.

She didn't sit for long, and before he was ready, she was up and looking out all the windows.

"I'm glad you think so." He went over to be closer to her so he could point out some areas of interest, at least that's what he told himself, when in fact he just wanted to be near her. He couldn't figure out this crazy attraction he was feeling toward her. But he didn't fight it.

Instead he started pointing out the cave area, and where some of the ships had sunk. Then he turned them toward the town and pointed out the places they had been and some other's he thought she might like to see.

She commented on each thing he pointed out and didn't seem to mind him being up close, in fact he could swear she'd snuggled back into him while he pointed over her shoulder. When he was finished showing her the sights, he talked about the current light and what it had been like before.

"When we get finished up here, we can go down and look in the museum, there are lots of older fixtures down there."

"It's so pretty up here, I could stay all day."

She was still in his arms so he had to agree that would be pleasant indeed.

She sighed, "But we don't want Jimmy locking us in here for the night, so I suppose we should carry on."

"If we must," he teased.

CHAPTER SIX

Gideon escorted her back down to the museum that had some of the old fixtures, and he explained how they'd worked in the past, she was a very good listener and asked insightful questions, so he droned on.

He hoped she wasn't being polite and was really interested. He talked about how they'd managed the light in the old days with someone spending the night in the tower to make sure the light was always lit. On dark rainy days they would keep it going twenty-four hours a day. Trading off the chore of watching over the light.

Gideon pointed out interesting little objects with tidbits of information about what they were for. He was worried she might get bored, but as soon as he started to hurry along, she stopped him with more questions. So, he finally settled in and let her browse and poke while he imparted all his knowledge.

When they were finished in the history museum he called out. "Jimmy! We're leaving now."

Jimmy appeared as if by magic, the kid was a little creepy sometimes. "Okay, Gideon, have a good day."

Patty Anne gushed, "Thanks so much, for letting us poke around. It really is all very fascinating."

Jimmy's ears turned red and Gideon took her arm to steer her out. Jimmy wasn't used to West Coast enthusiasm.

ONCE THEY WERE OUT IN THE SUNSHINE, PATTY ANNE couldn't contain her curiosity one minute longer. "So, how come you know every little bit about the lighthouse? Even down to what a particular screw is for and what each little piece of metal does. Is it a family thing? Is everyone that's part of the family required to know that?"

Gideon laughed. "Not at all. That would be silly. However, every class from kindergarten to twelfth grade has a field trip, every year, to the lighthouse. When we were kids it was really fun because we could run around. See what it looked like, run up and down the stairs. Plus, it's so much fun because it's so new and it's so different."

He sighed and shook his head. "But as we got older. The tests started coming. First it was simple things. What does the light look like, draw a picture of it? How does it work, label the parts? How did it look in the past, how did the people keep it on? But then as we got older, each year, they would find something new to make us learn. So, we had to go through the history museum with a fine-toothed comb and learn the name and the function of every single little thing. And then the teachers tested us on it."

He shuddered like it was abhorrent. "They've been using those same tests for years and years, so it's easy for them, but for the students, it's horrible, and crazy."

Patty Anne gaped. "You mean to tell me that every single

person in this town, that grew up here, knows all that about the lighthouse?"

Gideon nodded sadly. "Yes, I do. And believe me it's not something anyone would want to learn."

Patty Anne shrugged. "Well I found it quite fascinating. But yeah, I have to agree, I wouldn't want to know every tiny little crumb of detail about how a lighthouse works and what each piece of equipment does. Did you hold back some of your knowledge?"

Gideon patted her arm. "Yes, no one wants all the details, believe me, you'd have gotten a whole hell of a lot more information if I told you everything. Nobody wants to know all that, even those of us that grew up here. But it doesn't matter, we all do. It's all hardwired into our brains, so that we could pass those stupid tests every year."

Patty Anne realized the day might not have been fun for him. "So, the lighthouse isn't very fun for you to visit. I'm sorry."

He shook his head. "Well sure it is, it's still part of history, my history. Plus, it's fun to see it afresh through your eyes as opposed to the poor children that trudged through there year after year after year. I mean think about it, thirteen years of coming to the lighthouse. There's just not that much information, or that much interest."

"So, did you have to memorize other stuff, like all the ships that sank and all the people that came off the boats, and that kind of thing?"

He chuckled. "Oh yeah. That was another piece of history that we all got to learn. The teachers would say that it was important to know our history. Well, I don't think it's important to know every single sailor that came through here. Or whether they were legitimate, or whether they were pirates, whether they were drug runners, or slave ships. It's ridiculous."

Patty Anne laughed. "Oh, you really did hold back when you wrote your history book."

"Nobody wants all those little bits of information, and crap. I picked the most interesting sailors who crashed on our shores and I told those stories. Of course, Gideon McKeith was a fascinating fellow, so he was added in as the great guardian of the town."

She laughed. "So, when I asked you what bits of information you didn't put in your book, and you said, nothing. You were referring to the exciting stuff, you put all the noteworthy pieces in and kept all the boring scraps away."

"Well, yeah. Guilty as charged."

"Good for you. Nobody wants to read a bunch of boring material. So, you are the descendant of the Scotsman who saved the town from the smugglers and thieves, correct?"

Gideon shrugged. "One of many. The man was prolific, and it's been three hundred years."

"But you're the one named after him."

"There's been many Gideons in the town over the years, both from the family and not. And my mother was fanciful and wanted to name her first born after the legend. I have a distant cousin named Gideon also, fortunately his family lives in Boston."

Patty Anne laughed. "Does the broadsword still exist?"

"It does, but it's been stripped of it's jewels. One jewel given to each family, about a hundred years ago."

here were still several hours of daylight left, so Gideon said, "We can drive a little farther up the coast, and then park and go see the caves if you want."

"Oh goody. Let's do that."

"All right. I'll tell you about some of the creepier people that supposedly used the caves and what they used them for."

Patty Anne grinned. "Sounds good to me. Let's go."

The drive up the coast wasn't far, but it was beautiful, Gideon always liked it and by the sounds Patty Anne was making she was enjoying it too.

Before they reached their destination, she asked, "Are we going to run into Love Rock?"

"God, no. The pilgrims to that ridiculous farce wouldn't trouble themselves to come this far. It's right in town, the access is on the street that runs behind your B&B, maybe half a block away. The walk down to the shore where it sits is not quite as long as this is, but it's still at the bottom of the cliff the town sits on."

"So, you've been to it?"

"Sure, but it's just a rock. It has a bit of a shimmer to it, probably some flecks in the rock. I didn't get close enough to examine it."

Patty Anne chuckled. "Didn't want to get too close, just in case."

He started to deny it, on principle, but changed his mind. "I was in high school and no where near a permanent relationship."

Patty Anne shivered dramatically. "I never have understood the draw of getting married at eighteen."

"Regular sex. Only possible reason."

She laughed and poked him. "Cynical much?"

He gave her a wolfish grin. "We're here."

He drove into a little clearing and parked the car. "I have a couple of battery powered lanterns that we can take along to explore. We don't want to be beholden to the weather like in the old days."

She chuckled. "Yeah. Wouldn't want some gust of wind to blow out our lanterns and leave us trapped in the dark with no way to move."

"Exactly. One for you and one for me, and I'm gonna put this flashlight in my pocket, never hurts to have backup."

Next to where he parked was a path that led from the bluff the car sat on, down to the rocky shore. The ocean lapped a dozen yards further out. It wasn't a steep descent since there were a few switch backs to flatten the walk. When they got down to the rocky shore, Gideon led the way further north.

He said, "The first cave isn't too far, just around this little bend here."

When they got around to the mouth of the cave, they switched on their lanterns then held them out to peer inside. The light didn't go far into the murky darkness, but it was enough to see that there was nothing inside that they needed to be concerned about. So, they went in.

He showed her where they had played as kids. Beyond the prying eyes of the adults. When they got older, they might sneak a beer, or kiss a girl. Sometimes they came just to be alone and think. She saw evidence of inhabitants from the past. A couple of crates that could be sat on, a blackened clear spot where fire had once burned toward the mouth of the cave.

Some of the kids had scratched their names on the walls, some clever artists had drawn pictures of various exploits. Patty Anne chuckled looking at the scratchings on the wall.

She asked, "Is any of the artwork yours?"

Gideon shook his head. "No. I was never one to scribble on walls. But give me a piece of paper, and I'll go to town."

When she was finished examining everything, they went on to the next, which was deeper, bigger, and further underground. This one had evidence of being used in the less recent past. There were a few big barrels, what they'd had in them, she had no idea. They were empty now, some of them broken up. She let her imagination soar. Imagining barrels of whisky or guns.

They went on to the next cave which was about the same size, and this one Gideon had a story about. A slave ship had sunk off the coast and they'd managed to all make it to shore. At the far back of the cave there did seem to be some kind of jail-like structure, with some metal pegs hammered into the walls. It looked like they had tried to continue to hold the slaves.

He said, "In case a new ship could be found, to continue the journey."

"I think being held at the back of the cave would be horrible. My worst nightmare."

Gideon assured her, "Rumor is that the slaves had broken free, since there were more slaves alive than captors, they'd overpowered the guards. I don't think any stayed in the area, but had gone north, south, or even west."

"Good for them." She glanced back and shuddered at the thought of being enslaved at the back of the cave where it was so dark, and dank. It was no wonder they fought to get out as quickly as possible. She was happy to leave that cave and the grim reminder of man's cruelty to man.

The sunshine felt good on her face as they walked on. The next cave was nearly an underground house. There was a main area and then several smaller rooms off from that.

She asked Gideon, "Do you think it's natural or did someone dig into the walls to make the rooms?"

He shrugged. "It does seem to be almost a house. Maybe it was the murdering pirate, Captain Black's, house. I've never thought about it before, whether it was dug out."

"If pirates crashed on shore, they might know they wouldn't be welcome in town."

He nodded. "But how they would survive, would be the big question. Did they go into town and steal from people? Did they mostly live from the sea offerings? Did they get enough of their goods ashore that they could survive for a while? It's an interesting idea."

So, they made up stories of various scenarios, getting more ridiculous with each tale, that had them howling with laughter. By the time they'd finished with that cave, the tide was starting to come in, and it was getting close to dinnertime.

Gideon said, "I think that's all we've got time for today."

"How many more caves are there?"

"Oh lots, a couple dozen. I'm not sure I've seen all of them. They just keep going on up the coast."

"I hope I'll have time to come back and see a few more, but this is enough for today."

"I'm ready to go back and maybe find something to eat. What do you think?"

"I could eat."

"Well, let's see, you've been to the Dolphin Run. And you've been to the Lobster Hut. There's a nice restaurant behind the library, want to check it out with me?"

"Okay. I'd be happy to have dinner with you."

"Great."

CHAPTER EIGHT

Gideon and Patty Anne settled into a routine. Gideon played tour guide as they ventured further afield from his hometown. She'd never been to the east coast, so he had a wonderful time showing her all his favorite spots. Nothing was too far away, just a quick drive, so she got to see the states north, up to Maine, and south, down to Delaware.

With one day spent in New York City, which was way too crazy for her, but Gideon insisted she couldn't come all the way across the country and not see it, plus the nation's Capital, and Philadelphia. She loved seeing the Liberty Bell, and the White House, and so many other iconic places, even Time's Square, for a few minutes.

He talked her into spending the night in one of the luxurious hotels on Broadway. They'd both tucked a bag into his car when they started exploring further afield, just in case they might need to spend a night.

They walked up to the desk.

"How may I help you sir, madam?"

Gideon said, "We'd like two—"

She interrupted, "One room."

Gideon glanced at her but didn't argue. "One suite facing Broadway."

The desk clerk didn't bat an eye but handed them room cards.

When they were out of hearing distance Gideon asked, "Are you sure about sharing a room?"

"Very. I know I'm only here another week, but I want to be with you Gideon."

He kissed her softly as they waited for the elevator. "Music to my ears."

They rode up in the elevator, holding hands but staring straight ahead, she knew if they did any more than that they'd end up wrapped around each other like teenagers. She decided Gideon felt the same since he didn't try to make conversation.

When they reached their floor and found their room, her nerves made themselves known, so while Gideon switched on lights and set their bags on the dresser, she went over to look out the window pulling back the sheer curtain to view the streets below. Patty Anne saw the flashing lights on the buildings and looked down to see the crowds on the streets.

The crowds were much more interesting with her far above them. They nearly looked like ants scurrying around. She felt Gideon come up behind her and put his hands on her shoulders.

"We don't have to do anything if you're not feeling like it. We can do whatever we want, go see a show, hang out and watch movies. I'm happy just to be with you."

She sighed, how easily he could read her moods. She turned in his arms letting the sheer curtain drop from her hand. "I do want to make love, I'm just feeling nervous, remembering my breasts aren't as perky as they once were, my skin has a bit of a sag—"

Gideon interrupted her with a searing kiss. He continued kissing her until all the tension fled her body and she clung to him for support. Then he pulled back and whispered, "I want you Patty Anne, not some perky teenager. Just you."

She looked in his eyes and saw truth there. She nodded.

Then his mouth was on hers again, and she hardly noticed as he steered her toward the enormous bed. When the backs of her legs bumped into it, he slowly lowered her to the mattress with his strong hard body covering half of hers.

The long drugging kisses continued, he seemed to be in no hurry to take it any further. She was melting, her bones had no substance, her muscles no strength. Her body was flooded with sensation, simply from his mouth on hers.

Patty Anne barely felt the whisper of his hands over her body as his mouth stayed steadily plundering hers. The touches were light but potent on her neck, her shoulders, her breasts, continuing down to her waist and hips. Eddies of sensation whirled wherever he touched, and they were still fully dressed.

She yearned for skin, so she willed strength back into her arms and pulled at his shirt. He yanked the polo shirt over his head and tossed it away. She heard him growl in pleasure as her fingers ran across his flesh, her nails slightly scoring.

GIDEON'S HOLD ON HIS LUST SLIPPED WHEN PATTY ANNE touched his heated chest. While she tormented him, he let his hands remove her clothing in return. He pulled at the blouse trying not to tear it off her in a frenzy. Instead he managed to get the buttons undone, pulling the sides apart, he felt her tremble as he touched her with shaking hands.

She pushed him up and tore the blouse from her body, flinging it across the room. Then undid her bra and sent it flying after the same path. Once she was bared to him, she pulled him back down on top of her and squirmed, so their chests rubbed together.

The pleasure was so intense he thought his eyes might roll back in his head, but then she moaned and his focus was back on her, his hands seeking her breasts, rubbing his thumbs over her nipples until they furled into tight peaks. They might not be as firm as they had been in her youth, but they were responsive to his touch, and by the reaction he assumed they were still just as sensitive.

He lowered his head to suckle and her hands went into his hair, keeping him right where she wanted him. He was happy to exploit each breast until her breath was unsteady. His own breathing wasn't any better and he was hard as a rock.

His mouth found hers once again, but he felt her tugging at his pants. He looked her in the eyes. Her's had gone dark with lust. "Want to move this along, sweetheart?"

"Yes, get rid of those pants, Gideon."

He gave her a sly grin. "I will if you will."

"Yes, hurry."

They moved away from each other both moving fast to remove their remaining clothing. She beat him and laid back on the bed, opening her legs so he could slip between them. A thought struck him. "I don't have any protection, Sweetheart."

"I'm past childbearing and haven't been with anyone in years."

"I haven't been with anyone in about five years."

Her smile was potent. "Good enough, now let's continue."

"You sure? I'm sure the hotel has some."

"Yes, I'm sure. Now, Gideon."

He climbed back on the bed between her legs, but decided he'd make sure she was plenty wet enough and put his mouth on her most sensitive area. It didn't take long to send her flying and she was fully wet when he went back up her body and guided his cock into her still throbbing channel. The heat and wet surrounded him and he groaned in pleasure.

She clung to him with arms and legs and he started to love her with long smooth strokes. He knew that wouldn't last long as the tension grew in his body, but he hoped he could prolong her orgasm or maybe even heighten it.

She clutched onto his shoulders, her nails digging in. "Faster, Gideon, harder."

He complied, trying to hold on but she squeezed him with her inner muscles, and he flew as his body emptied into hers. She heard him call out her name and he buried his head in her neck and hair.

When he could move again, he rolled off of her drawing her with him, so she landed on top.

She chuckled and pulled the blankets over the top of them. "That was a sooth move."

"I didn't want to squish you."

She squeezed his arm. "You are solidly built. You must do something to keep in shape, an author's life can be sedentary."

"I like to keep in shape, besides when I run, or work out, it frees my mind and ideas flow better. I keep my phone handy and dictate into it when the plots won't wait. In the shower I have a pencil and waterproof paper."

"Clever, whoever invented those are probably wealthy people."

He ran his hand down her back, enjoying the smooth, soft skin. "Yeah, those and the sticky note inventors."

"Oh, yeah. I have every color in the rainbow and fun shapes too."

"When I first started writing I used them to help me plot my books. I could move them all around as I thought through the different plot points. I use more of an outline these days, because my brain is now conditioned to think of the plot as a whole, so I don't do much rearranging. But I still color code the outline. It makes it easy to see where something is missing, a quick glance shows when one color is light or too heavy."

"Maybe you can show me some time—it sounds fascinating."

He kissed her forehead, he didn't think it was fascinating, but it would be new to her, so something different and interesting. "I would be happy to show you. I still have some old plotting boards around; I can show you the newbie way and the current process."

"That would be fun. I always want to learn more of the writing process."

She was adorable. He couldn't get enough of her. "Want to go take a bath in that enormous bathtub?"

"That would be fun. I hope it has jets."

"I'm sure it does."

The tub did indeed have jets and they spent a relaxed hour in the hot frothing water. Later they cuddled on the bed and watched old movies, with some snacks from room service. He'd rarely had a more enjoyable evening.

CHAPTER NINE

*H*er vacation flew by. Every day bringing them closer to parting ways. Patty Anne didn't want to admit it, even to herself, but she'd fallen in love with Gideon and it was going to break her heart to leave him.

But she had a home and a job to get back to. So tomorrow she would board the plane and have memories to sustain her. Maybe they could talk on the phone and remain friends. Or simply let the feelings fade. They'd decided tonight they would go out to a fancy restaurant that had music and dancing.

But she had the afternoon to herself since he was doing some business catchup with his agent and publisher. She decided to go down to see the famous Love Rock, it seemed silly to go, but she knew herself and she would regret not going. Since it was so close, she walked.

There were a few signs pointing the way. Nothing big or ostentatious, but enough to keep a person from getting lost. When she rounded the corner, she saw the large rock sitting next to the small beach. It seemed to shimmer in the sunshine.

She told herself it was probably from mica in its makeup.

But it was a sight to see and she did seem drawn to it. She walked up and ran her hand along the surface. Up close she didn't see any mica, it just looked like a normal rock to her.

Patty Anne stood with her hand on the rock and looked out over the ocean. Thoughts and memories of Gideon assailed her. She was going to miss him. They had one night left together and then they would part company in the morning.

She was looking forward to dancing after they ate. Just to be in his arms. After standing at the rock for a long time, she decided one more trip to Treasures of the Deep was in order, to see what else she might want. But a stop at the library was needed too. She'd made some friends here and she wanted to say goodbye.

Jennifer squealed when she walked in and Patty Anne gave her the librarian scowl and shushed her. Then they both laughed because the library was empty except for the two of them.

"I leave tomorrow."

"I know. I'm going to miss you."

Patty Anne swallowed to keep the tears at bay. "We can still keep in touch. You should take a vacation and come to Chedwick."

"I can try to talk my hubby into it, but he's not fond of flying. He's always certain the plane is going to drop out of the sky and kill everyone."

With a grin Patty Anne said, "Ah, one of those. Always the big strong guys."

"Yeah. I don't tease him too much."

They talked for a few more minutes and then hugged one another when the kids started showing up for reading hour. Patty Anne went on to the shop, thinking she was going to miss more than Gideon when she left.

Patty Anne managed to keep her purchases small so they would fit in her suitcase. Martie had been excited to see her again and had helped her pick out some small items. She'd already bought an extra bag to get everything back, she wasn't about to buy too much.

When she got back to the bed and breakfast, she was pleased to see she had enough time to get ready for her date with Gideon, but not too much time to get melancholy. She dressed up in the one fancy dress she'd brought with her and carefully applied makeup, and selected jewelry that would enhance.

She met Gideon in the parlor of the Bed and Breakfast, he looked amazing in a navy-blue suit and pinstriped shirt, his royal blue tie had a pattern, that she couldn't decipher, until she got close. It had books on it. She laughed. "Where did you get that tie?"

"My publisher, actually. They found it quite amusing, but I have to admit I love it."

"I like it too! What could possibly be better for an author, than books?"

"Exactly." He took her hand. "You look amazing. I'm having dinner with the prettiest woman in six states."

She laughed. "Well since your states are miniscule that's not saying a whole lot."

He grinned and drew her out the door, to his car. Once she was settled, he went around to his own door while she tried not to be sad that this was their last time together.

GIDEON WAS FEELING ANTSY. HE HAD PROMISED HIMSELF HE would wait until after dinner to give her his gift. But he didn't want to wait, he wanted to see her wearing it. When he slid into the driver's seat, he turned on the overhead light. And pulled the box out of his suit coat pocket.

"I have something I want to give you. I was going to wait until later, but I want to see it on you."

"Oh Gideon, that's not necessary."

"I know, but you are the only person I have ever wanted to give this to. So, I'm afraid you'll have to accept it."

He opened the box and held it out to her.

She gasped. "Is this what I think it is?" A beautiful aquamarine necklace laid on a bed of black velvet.

Gideon shrugged. "I've had the stone my entire life. I believe it is our family's gem from the sword's hilt. I had it made into a necklace for you."

"But it's a family heirloom, you can't give it to me. It is mine to do with as I wish. I want you to have it."

She held it up and the light shimmered through it. "It's so beautiful."

"I've always thought so. Will you wear it and remember me?"

She looked at him with tears in her eyes. "I will. I will never forget you and it has nothing to do with the necklace. I love you, Gideon. I will miss you fiercely."

He helped her fasten it on her neck. "I love you too, Patty Anne. I can come visit you, and we can talk on the phone often."

"I would love to show you around eastern Washington. Do try to come out."

He leaned over the console and she did too. Their lips met and they exchanged a soft, reverent kiss. She pulled back and he could see fire in her eyes.

"I think we better get to the restaurant," he said with a sigh.

She whispered, "Yes."

They ate and talked and danced the night away. He loved holding her in his arms and he reveled in the fact she was wearing his most prized possession. They tried to keep the evening from ending but they finally admitted defeat when they were the only customers left and the staff had started cleaning up.

They went back to her room and spent the night together, making slow sweet love, and in the morning their love making was frantic. He wanted to imprint her on his brain, their kisses and caresses were searing. When they came together it was an explosion of feelings that he tried to use to hide the fact that she was leaving in a few hours.

He didn't know how he was going to go on with her so very far away. He'd come to rely on her joy and enthusiasm for life. Returning to his real life didn't hold an appeal. He knew he would still write but now it seemed so lonely.

CHAPTER TEN

atty Anne pulled her attention back to her job, away from daydreaming as she stroked the stone of the necklace she wore every day. Daydreaming about Gideon. She'd been back in Chedwick a month and she still missed him. It seemed like every minute of the day she thought of him. They talked nearly every night, long conversations about how her reading programs were faring, what new books she was getting in, and how his writing was going, his battle with the publisher to produce a six-book series.

She'd not heard from him in two days and it was killing her. He'd gone to New York to talk to both his agent and publisher. He was determined to write the six-book series and if his publisher didn't agree with that, he was willing to walk. Either to another publisher, or he'd also given self-publishing a thought.

Patty Anne was dying to hear how it went and hoped he would have time to call her tonight. She went back to entering the books the kids were reading into her spreadsheet. The mini treasure chests were a hit, and the checkouts of pirate stories had skyrocketed.

She heard the bell on the door chime and looked up. She shook her head and rubbed her eyes before looking back. It wasn't a mirage; it really was Gideon standing just inside the door with a huge grin on his face. She jumped up and charged into his arms, knocking him back a step, and squeezed him tight.

"I didn't know you were coming, why didn't you tell me?" she scolded.

"I wanted it to be a surprise."

"But I didn't arrange for any time off."

"You don't need to. I'm going to be hanging around for a while."

"A while? How long?"

He shrugged. "As long as I like. I have six books to write about this area, I'll need to do a lot of research."

"But…"

"No buts, I want to spend more time with you."

She laid her head on his shoulder. "I want to spend more time with you, too. But what about your house? And everything?"

"It doesn't matter. I wandered around town for a week trying to get back to normal, the only highlight of my day was talking to you on the phone. I even went down to that stupid Love Rock and just stared out to sea. That's when I knew something had to change. So, I put my house with the real estate agent to lease it or use as a vacation rental. I have a truck on its way with all the things I want with me. I have my laptop for now, so I can work."

"You said six books. Did you convince your publisher?"

"My agent and I laid out a proposal they would have been foolish to refuse. The fact that my agent dropped the name of another publisher interested in me didn't hurt."

She laughed. "Good for you."

"So, are you staying in one of the hotels?"

"Yes, until I find a place to rent. I've got Kyle Moore looking for something."

"If my place wasn't so small…"

"I know, but we're not ready for that yet. We need to get to know each other better."

SIX MONTHS LATER, GIDEON PACED HIS LIVING ROOM. HE HAD a date with Patty Anne, but not for an hour. He'd been ready for thirty minutes and still had an hour to wait.

He'd turned in the first of his six stories, the first one had practically written itself, once he'd gotten to Chedwick and had met the inhabitants. He doubted the rest would flow so easily. He'd been thrilled with the first one and decided it was one of his best. A change of scenery had worked wonders, that, or spending a lot of time with Patty Anne.

He'd also made friends with the children's book author and they met regularly to talk plots and marketing. Both of them wrote for a large publishing house, but the days of the publishers doing all the marketing were long gone. Authors had to be on social media, make appearances, and even run some ads. It was a little disconcerting to both of them, since they'd both been publishing during the golden years.

The published photographer joined them occasionally when they were talking strictly marketing, she didn't need the plotting conversations. She had a couple of coffee table type books out that were gorgeous, so every so often she wanted to stir the pot to see if she could find new audiences for her books.

His mind turned away from books and back to Patty Anne, they'd spent nearly every day of the last six months together, at least for a few minutes. Having a meal together or just chatting about their work. On her days off she'd taken him to some of the surrounding towns. He'd loved the little Bavarian-esque village of Leavenworth. They'd had brats and beer and had toured the many shops along the main street. They'd gone back for Octoberfest and that had been a real treat, with dancers performing, and street fairs.

She'd taken him to see the apple production in Wenatchee and they'd toured the Applets and Cotlets factory in Cashmere. When she could take a day or two off, they'd gone further afield, and they'd had the best time. They had maintained both a friendship and a love affair. He was ready to move things forward, and he hoped she was too.

He'd find out soon enough. He looked at the clock, only twenty minutes to go, he'd made reservations in the fine dining side of Amber's restaurant and had requested a bottle of champagne, just in case they had something to celebrate. Dear God, he hoped they would be celebrating.

He couldn't wait any longer and walked slowly out to his car. In his driveway stood the town peacock in full array. He spoke to the bird, "I love that you're here to bring me luck."

The bird ruffled his feathers as if to say, "What else would I be doing here in the middle of winter?"

Gideon chuckled and got in his car.

Then he drove as slowly as he could to her house and was still five minutes early. He didn't know whether to wait in the car and look like a stalker, or just go to her door early. He finally decided on the latter and walked slowly to her door.

She opened it with a frown. "What are you doing? Pretending to be a snail?"

"I'm early."

She rolled her eyes. "Not that early. Come on in, while I grab my coat and purse."

She looked lovely in her fire engine red dress. Her hair was in a sleek bob with a small amount of makeup. Except for her mouth, which matched the dress, and he wanted to kiss that red lipstick right off of her. *Patience*, he told himself.

She brought her warm black coat with the faux fur lining. He helped her into it and breathed in her fragrance, she smelled delightful. He suppressed a shiver of anticipation and escorted her out to his car. "You look magnificent, by the way."

"You look pretty good yourself," she said so softly, he almost didn't hear her.

When they got to the restaurant, they were escorted back to the table he had requested. The centerpiece of red roses he'd ordered almost looked like they belonged there, but not quite.

"Oh, look at the pretty roses. Did you request them, or did we just get the lucky table?"

Rather than answer he took her hand. "Patty Anne, we've known each other for almost eight months. Every one of those days with you has been delightful. I love you and want to continue to spend every day with you."

He got up and came around to her side of the table and knelt. "Patty Anne, would you do me the very great honor of becoming my wife?"

Patty Anne sighed. "I thought you would never ask. Yes, Gideon I would be thrilled to marry you. I love you, so very much."

He grinned and opened the ring box he'd had in a pocket. Inside was an aquamarine ring surrounded by diamonds. "It's not an heirloom, but..."

"I love it."

He slid the ring on her finger and kissed some of that

bright red lipstick off her mouth, before returning to his seat.

Once he was seated Amber appeared with the bottle of champagne. "I see we have something to celebrate."

Patty Anne grinned and held out her hand. "We do, indeed."

Amber oohed and awed over the ring and then poured them both a flute of the sparkling wine.

They clinked their glasses together, and he said, "To a match made in heaven. This lucky author has a lovely lady librarian to love."

She laughed and they talked about the future, as they ate an exquisite meal, basking in the love they had for one another.

THE END

This series continues with Hello Again a novella containing Janet and Everitt's story (previously found in the Goodbye Doesn't Mean Forever Anthology).
If you enjoyed this story, please leave a review on your favorite retailer, Bookbub, or Goodreads.
Thanks so much!

Ted and Tammy's story

The Author's Lady Librarian: Lake Chelan #11

Patty Anne and Gideon's story

The Fire Chief's Surprise: Lake Chelan #12

Greg and Sandy's short story

Hello Again: Lake Chelan #13

Janet and Everett's story

(Previously part of the Goodbye Doesn't Mean Forever anthology)

Three's a Crowd: Lake Chelan #14

Kyle and Samantha's story

(Previously part of the Valentine Kisses anthology)

BURLAP AND BARBED WIRE SERIES

Colorado Cowboys

A Cowboy for Alyssa: Burlap and Barbed Wire #1

Beau and Alyssa's story

Taming Adam: Burlap and Barbed Wire #2

Adam and Rachel's story

Tempting Chase: Burlap and Barbed Wire #3

Chase and Katie's story

Roping Cade: Burlap and Barbed Wire #4

Cade and Summer's story

Trusting Drew: Burlap and Barbed Wire #5

Drew and Lily's story

Emma's Rodeo Cowboy: Burlap and Barbed Wire #6

Emma and Zach's story

SADDLES AND SECRETS SERIES

Wyoming Wranglers

The Lawman: Saddles and Secrets #1

Maggie Ann and John's story

The Watcher: Saddles and Secrets #2

Christina and Rob's story

The Rescuer: Saddles and Secrets #3

Milly and Tim's story

The Vacation: Saddles and Secrets Short Story #4

Andrea and Carl Ray's story

(Previously Part of the Getting Wild in Deadwood anthology)

The Neighbor: Saddles and Secrets #5

Terri and Rafe's story

HELLUVA ENGINEER SERIES

Helluva Engineer: Helluva Engineer #1

Patricia and Steve's story

Christmas at the Rockin' K: Helluva Engineer #2

Brenda and Thomas's story

Her Forever Man: Helluva Engineer #3

Tracy and Lloyd's story

What does a geeky math nerd know about writing romance?

That's a darn good question. As a former techy I've done everything from computer programming to international trainer. Prior to college I had lots of different jobs and activities that were so diverse, I was an anomaly.

None of that qualifies me for writing novels. But I have some darn good stories to tell and a lot of imagination.

I have lived in Colorado, Hawaii and currently reside in Washington. Going from two states with 340 days of sun to a state with 340 days of clouds, I had to do something to perk me up. And that's when I started this new adventure called author. Joining the Romance Writers of America and two local chapters, helped me learn the craft quickly and was a ton of fun.

My family consists of two grown children, their spouses, two adorable grand-daughters, and one grand dog. My favorite activity is playing with my granddaughters!

When the girls can't play with their amazing grand-mother, my interests are reading and writing, yay! I started reading at a young age with the Nancy Drew mysteries and have continued to be an avid reader my whole life. My favorite reading material is romance, but occasionally if other stories creep into my to-be-read pile, I don't kick them out.

Some of the strange jobs I have held are a carnation grow-er's worker, a trap club puller, a pizza hut waitress, a software engineer, an international trainer, and a business program manager. I took welding, drafting and upholstery in high school, a long time ago, when girls didn't take those classes, so I have an eclectic bunch of knowledge and experience.

And for something really unusual… I once had a raccoon as a pet.

Join with me as I tell my stories, weaving real tidbits from my life in with imaginary ones. You'll have to guess which is which. It will be a hoot!

Contact me:

www.shirleypenick.com
To sign up for Shirley's Monthly Newsletter, sign up on my website or send email to shirleypenick@outlook.com, subject newsletter.

Follow me:

facebook.com/ShirleyPenickAuthorFans

twitter.com/shirley_penick

instagram.com/shirleypenickauthor

goodreads.com/shirleypenick

bookbub.com/authors/shirley-penick